Bible
Critters

SPIDERS!

To a disciple,

Happy Reading!

Pat Matuszak

Zonder**kidz**

Zonderkidz.

The children's group of Zondervan

www.zonderkidz.com

Bible Critters: Spiders
Copyright © 2002 by Pat Matuszak
Illustrations copyright © 2002 by David Sheldon

Requests for information should be addressed to:
Zonderkidz, Grand Rapids, Michigan 49530

ISBN: 0-310-70812-5

Editor: Gwen Ellis
Interior Design: Michelle Lenger

Printed in China
04 05 06 07/LP/4 3 2 1

Written by **Pat Matuszak**

Illustrated by **David Sheldon**

To Christi, the spider-whomper, Janet, the spider-sweeper, Connie, the spider-stomper, Gwen, the tarantula-tamer, and to my great-grandma Inez Bell Ley, who felt the same way about spiders as Mrs. Noah!

P.M.

For William, Sarah, and Christopher

D.S.

The **hairy, creepy spider**
Hitched a ride onto the Ark.
He hid from Mrs. Noah
On a basket made of bark.

But even as he climbed aboard,
And as the rain came down,
He saw that bugs and spiders
Made Mrs. Noah frown.

As Mrs. Noah got her broom
And cleaned the tracked in dirt,
The hairy, creepy spider slipped
Way down in Noah's shirt!

When Mrs. Noah washed the shirt,
She found him in the pocket!
And when she aimed a swat at him,
He took off like a rocket!

He ran right up a rhino's horn
And down the other side.
He scurried through the snakes' room
To see where he could hide.

He hopped in with the bunnies.
She saw him try to play.
He hid inside the lion's mane.
She thought he'd gone away.

The **webby, wiggly spider**
was rolled up in a mat.
When Mrs. Noah saw him,
She chased him with a bat!

He ran into the tiger pit
And hung onto a tail,
But Mrs. Noah saw him
And chased him up the rail.

He tried to look like lashes
On a very tall giraffe,
But when Mrs. Noah saw him,
She didn't even laugh.

He jumped onto the ceiling
And slipped out to the deck.
He hid behind the elephant
When she came out to check.

"We should be nice to spiders,"
Mrs. Noah's three sons cried.
"God said two of everything
Aboard our boat should ride!"

"Bats and snakes and mice have come,
And they are all behaving."
But critters with eight hairy legs
Set Mrs. Noah raving!

She was so very careful
To clean and sweep the place,
But shrieked when sticky spider webs
Would brush against her face.

She was so scared of spiders,
She couldn't just pretend
That a webby, fuzzy, crawly thing
Would ever be her friend.

She always had a candle
When she walked in the dark,
'Cause she felt very nervous
About bug-things on the Ark.

She didn't mind the chirping,
A bark or roaring sound,
But scritchy-scratchy footsteps
Made her stop and look around.

The leggy, lanky spider
Was hiding in some flowers.
She wasn't found by Noah's wife
For many, many hours.

But when she saw that spider's web,
She swept it with her broom.
So leggy lanky spider
Hid inside the monkeys' room.

The monkeys didn't tell a thing.
They let the spider hide,
So the spider told her spider friends,
"The apes are on our side."

The other spiders joined her,
Keeping webs far out of sight.
They'd eat the flies and gnats in there,
All through the dark of night!

The monkeys were the only ones
To get a good night's sleep—
'Cuz flies buzzed and bit and woke
The hippos, dogs, and sheep!

The flies began to multiply—
They buzzed both night and day.
Noah and the other creatures
Just wished they'd go away.

Then Mrs. Noah noticed that
The monkeys' room had none.
"It's the spiders in the corners,"
Declared her oldest son.

"They caught the flies in sticky webs,
And now this room is clean."
"Well, how about that!" said his mom.
"I see just what you mean."

"Their webs are really useful—
I see now why they're sticky.
I knocked down webs that God made good,
Because I thought them icky."

"Now I see why our God has said,
'Save two of every beast.'
He loves all things that he has made
Down to the very least."

"It just may be that I've been wrong
To chase them all away.
It looks like spiders have a job.
I think I'll let them stay!"

So all the creatures on the Ark
Were glad that she could see
That God had plans and jobs for them—
Just like for you and me!

Spooky Spider Stuff

People talk about spiders as if they were only gross, hairy, and disgusting; but they are really interesting—if you can get past the idea that you are looking at creatures who look back at you with two rows of eyes!

Crab spiders live in garden flowers and try to look like the flowers' petals. To catch their meals, they simply have to be still and wait. Before long insects will walk right into them, looking for flower nectar or places to land.

Spiders are good at construction.

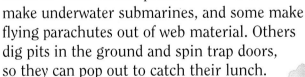

They construct many different kinds of webs. Some spiders make underwater submarines, and some make flying parachutes out of web material. Others dig pits in the ground and spin trap doors, so they can pop out to catch their lunch.

Spiders' webs aren't the only things that are sticky.

Their feet are made with special brushes that stick to walls and ceilings like suction cups.

Fishing spiders

live in swamp areas. They dangle their feet just under the water and catch tiny fish that come up to the surface to nibble.

Most spiders are good jumpers.

Since they have eight legs, they have a great springboard! The best jumpers can spring as far as forty times their body length!